137

Christopher's
Dream Car

by Andreas Greve

Annick Press,
Toronto Canada

Annick Press gratefully acknowledges the
support of The Canada Council and the Ontario
Arts Council.

Canadian Cataloguing in Publication Data

Greve, Andreas, 1953–
    Christopher's dream car

ISBN 1-55037-169-X (bound) ISBN 1-55037-166-5 (pbk.)

I. Title.

P27.G74Ch 1991   j823   C91-094242-0

Distributed in Canada and the USA by:
Firefly Books Ltd.
250 Sparks Avenue
Willowdale, Ontario
M2H 2S4

The art in this book has been rendered in
water colours
The text was set in Belwe by Attic Typesetting

∞ Printed in Canada on acid free paper
by D.W. Friesen & Sons

*In loving memory of
my grandparents*

Christopher's neighbourhood had lots of cars. They were parked all over the streets and driveways: large cars, smaller ones, trucks—and then there were those stunning, shiny, fabulous dream cars that would take you anywhere you wanted.

He would walk around them, polish a mirror with his sleeve and guess at their maximum speed.

Actually, Chris had a dream car of his own, except that it wasn't parked in front of his house, nor even in his town. It was his secret, because Chris was sure nobody would understand if he attempted to explain. Well, maybe his Grandpa would.
The only time he could drive his dream car was during summer vacation, when he went to visit his grandparents. He loved visiting them anyway: they had a cat, he was allowed to play outside all day, and his dream car was always waiting for him behind the barn.

He was a little impatient sitting next to his Grandpa who had picked him up at the railroad station, and just a bit eager to get away from Grandma's hugs and kisses—he raced outside, around the corner of the barn and there—

—sure enough, there it was in the same place as always. He walked
right around his dream car twice to check everything: okay,
nothing thrown in, nothing tossed out. Even the old crank sat in its
usual place (he needed it to start the motor). The heavy rubber sling
still held the driver's door in place.

After Chris' third attempt the motor went brrrram brrram. If he pushed all the right buttons the window washers would start and he could see for miles down the country road. He was about to go for a quick spin when he heard a voice: "Luuuuuuuunch time!" It was his Grandma, calling from the back yard. He ran to join them. He loved eating outside. And they would have his favourite dessert: stewed red berries with cream and chocolate chips on top!

As they finished, Grandpa said he would have to leave pretty soon
to take a load of tomatoes to the market.
"Oh, could we come along, pleaaaase, me and the cat?" pleaded
Chris. But Grandpa had no room. He was taking the neighbour, and
the back of the truck wasn't even big enough for all the tomatoes.
They had to leave a crate behind.
"The cat! Sorry Chris, there's not even room for a lady bug. Not this
time."

It was true. When the neighbour was finally settled under his parcels and baskets, you could barely see the tip of his nose. "Not to worry," Chris said to the cat, "we'll just have to go on our own then." "Make sure you're back in time for dinner," said Grandpa. Chris nodded and carried the heavy tomato crate to his car, placed the cat on the passenger seat, and turned the crank.

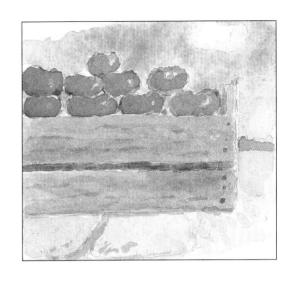

As they approached the town the road became very busy. There was a whole row of circus cars lined up, headed for a country fair. Chris noticed smoke pouring from a tractor stopped on the shoulder. A boy in a yellow T-shirt held out his hand.
"Could you tow me into town? My motor's pooped."

His name was Mario, and he crawled under the car with a very heavy rope.
"But don't go too fast," he warned, "or the merry-go-round will land in the ditch."
"Don't worry," said Chris, "I have to take it easy anyway, there's a load of tomatoes in the back for the market."
"Hey, have you ever thought of selling them one at a time? You make more money that way."
"One at a time. You mean like candied apples on a stick?"
"You got it, candied tomatoes," said Mario. Slowly, carefully, they went into town.

By the time they finished putting a popsicle stick into every tomato, the boys had maple syrup in their hair, on their elbows and behind their knees. The cat was almost stuck to the back seat.

The candied tomatoes were an instant hit. Some people said,
"Candied tomatoes? What a crazy idea," but then they bought one
or two anyway.

In the evening, when the music stopped, it turned colder and stars were in the sky. All the people had disappeared.

"Back home," Mario said, "it's much more fun at night. All the people come outside and have a good time and stay up for as long as they like."
"Is it far from here?" Chris asked.
"Very far," Mario replied.
"Sounds good. Let's go there," said Chris. And in no time they were ready and on their way.

The cat was asleep on the back seat as they drove into the night.

In the distance they could see the woods approaching. The road ran along high mountain rises and steep cliffs at times, and they even saw snowy peaks. But for a long time they didn't see a living thing. It would have been scary, except that Mario knew the way.

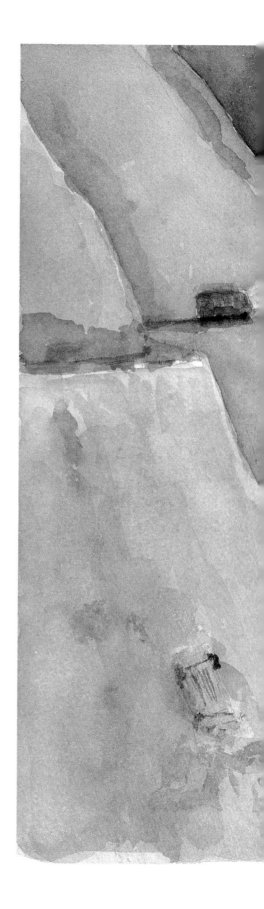

When the sun came up everything had changed, even the trees.
A shepherd was driving his herd across the road, so the boys had to
stop and wait. The lambs stared at them and sniffed the car. Chris
felt they were surrounded by a sea of wool. The shepherd said hello
as if he knew them, and as they entered the small town everybody
else seemed to know them, too.

Down by the harbour people treated them to a breakfast of french fries, lemonade and little doughnuts. A fisherman asked them if they could possibly row his boat, as his engine wouldn't start. He was the last one of the fleet.

"Sure thing," they said, "let's go."

Out in the high waves Chris helped the fisherman pull a heavy net aboard, while Mario managed to fix the engine with the help of a rusty nail and a piece of a shell.

"Unbelievable," said the fisherman happily. "It works even better than before." They were the first to come in. The boys were offered as much fish as they wanted, but they each took just one, for the cat.

They approached the car. Right away something seemed wrong. Christopher kept calling the cat, but she was nowhere to be seen, not under, nor on top, nor anywhere around the neighbourhood. They asked everybody and everybody gave them a different reply.

One child said that the cat was on the roof. They climbed up a
steep set of steps and ran and jumped from roof to roof. They
could see the whole town, the flower sellers and ice cream vendors,

the musicians preparing for the evening concert in the square, but no cat. Chris was very uneasy by now. What if something had happened to his grandparents' cat?

"Let's check the car again," he said, and sure enough, the cat had
returned safe and sound.
"Mario, I have to take her back pretty soon. My Grandmother
wouldn't be happy if I were late for dinner, but she would be
terribly upset if we lost her cat!"

"Do you really need to go?"
Mario asked sadly. "Will you find
the way?" "Of course," said Chris.
"Would you mind turning the
crank for me?"
Mario waved as Chris and the cat
drove out of town.

Somehow the narrow mountain
road looked unfamiliar as Chris
steered the car over rubble and
rocks.

The sun was going down, and suddenly it seemed like they were headed straight for the river.

"I'm afraid it's going to get a little wet, cat," said Chris, "you had better find a spot of high ground." He eased the car into the water and the motor began to cough dangerously. Slowly, the car headed for the shore.

Suddenly, the sun disappeared completely, and a heavy shadow fell across his face. The shadow was coughing and his grandfather stood in the door with a little smile.

"I thought I might find you back here. Time for dinner, Grandma's waiting," he said.

As they walked to the house Grandpa added, "Some car you've got there. I'll bet it takes you to pretty exciting places!" "You'd better believe it," said Chris, "but isn't it lucky that I always manage to come back just in time for dinner?"